THE MOON OF THE
BEARS

THE THIRTEEN MOONS

The Moon of the Owls (JANUARY)

The Moon of the Bears (FEBRUARY)

The Moon of the Salamanders (MARCH)

The Moon of the Chickarees (APRIL)

The Moon of the Monarch Butterflies (MAY)

The Moon of the Fox Pups (JUNE)

The Moon of the Wild Pigs (JULY)

The Moon of the Mountain Lions (AUGUST)

The Moon of the Deer (SEPTEMBER)

The Moon of the Alligators (OCTOBER)

The Moon of the Gray Wolves (NOVEMBER)

The Moon of the Winter Bird (DECEMBER)

The Moon of the Moles (DECEMBER–JANUARY)

NEW EDITION   THE THIRTEEN MOONS

THE MOON OF THE
BEARS

BY JEAN CRAIGHEAD GEORGE

ILLUSTRATED BY RON PARKER

HarperCollins*Publishers*

The illustrations in this book were painted
with Jo–sonya acrylic gouache on illustration board.

Library of Congress Cataloging-in-Publication Data
George, Jean Craighead, date
   The moon of the bears / by Jean Craighead George ; illustrated by
Ron Parker. — New ed.
      p.   cm. — (The Thirteen moons)
   Includes bibliographical references and index.
   Summary: Chronicles a year in a black bear's life, beginning with
her emerging from hibernation in Tennessee's Smoky Mountains
during the spring thaw in February.
   ISBN 0-06-022791-5. — ISBN 0-06-022792-3 (lib. bdg.)
   1. Bears—Juvenile literature. 2. Black bear—Great Smoky
Mountains (N.C. and Tenn.)—Juvenile literature. [1. Black bear.
2. Bears.] I. Parker, Ron, ill.   II. Title.   III. Series: George, Jean
Craighead, date,   Thirteen moons (HarperCollins)
QL795.B4G4   1993   91-22557
599.74'446—dc20   CIP
                                                                AC

Why is this series called The Thirteen Moons?

Each year there are either thirteen full moons or thirteen new moons. This series of books is named in their honor.

Our culture, which bases its calendar on sun-time, has no names for the thirteen moons. I have named the thirteen lunar months after thirteen North American animals. Primarily night prowlers, these animals, at a particular time of the year in a particular place, do wondrous things. The places are known to you, but the animal moon names are not because I made them up. So that you can place them on our sun calendar, I have identified them with the names of our months. When I ran out of these, I gave the thirteenth moon, the Moon of the Moles, the expandable name December-January.

Fortunately, the animals do not need calendars, for names or no names, sun-time or moon-time, they follow their own inner clocks.

—Jean Craighead George

IN FEBRUARY THE APPALACHIAN Mountains from Canada to Georgia were rigid with winter's ice and snow. And yet the great stone and earthen mountain range seemed to breathe. It breathed in with the thaw of day and out with the freeze of night. The breathing moved the sap up trees in the warmth of the sunlight and down again by the chill of the moon. The thaw and the freeze split rocks and eroded chasms, and it brought hibernating creatures to consciousness and put them back to sleep again.

February is the moon of awakening and sleeping, the moon of the bears. In their dens on mountainsides, in hollows, under logs, beside trees, they are coming slowly out of, and then sliding back into, their winter sleep. They are not alone in this. The plants and animals are all stirring and stopping under the moon of the bears.

A black bear was asleep in a shallow den under a fallen oak tree. The log lay in a Tennessee wilderness of hardwoods, conifers, and underbrush as dense as lawn grass. The hardwood trees were steel gray, their leafless twigs like icy webs. The limbs of the conifers—pine, hemlock, and spruce—drooped as if hugging themselves in the cold.

Around noon warm winds from the South blew into Tennessee, and the thaw began. The warmth remained for three days. A boulder near the bear snapped as the ice in its cracks let go. The snow began to melt and gurgle into the soil. The warmth reached the bear. Her heartbeat quickened. Her breathing came faster.

She opened her eyes.

Growling softly, she lifted her big, doglike head from her furry belly. Although she had not eaten since October, she still wore much of the thick layer of fat she had laid down in summer. It kept her perfectly warm in her icy saucer under the log. The leaves and sticks that covered her had sealed into a cocoon-like blanket by drifting snow. She matched the floor of the forest so well that not even the curious blue jays knew she was there.

The bear wheezed and lifted her head higher, further cracking her cocoon. She sniffed. Her eyesight was quite poor, but her nose was so keen she could smell the sap moving up the maples and birches and the scent of people three miles away. She could also smell delicious white grubs inside her three-foot-thick log.

She was one of more than a hundred thousand black bears that live in dense woods near meadows and swamps of Florida; of the Appalachian

and Rocky mountains; of California, Oregon, and Washington; and of Canada and Alaska to the Arctic Circle. Black bears like to live close to people, visiting towns to take hot dogs from grills or to walk through backyards and down highways. Black bears, unlike grizzlies, won't attack humans unless they are cornered or separated from their cubs by an ignorant person. They are not wilderness bears like the grizzly and polar bears, although they will live there. They prefer the woods near suburbia, farms, and orchards where their favorite foods abound. In recent years more and more black bears have been seen strolling in view of people as hunters put down their guns and pick up their cameras.

A black bear is also cinnamon brown, gray, creamy tan, silver-blue, and even white. The "white" black bear makes its home on Gribble Island near British Columbia. All the differently colored black bears are one species, *Ursus americanus*. The grizzly bear, *Ursus arctos*, is three to four times bigger, less tolerant of humans, and nearly extinct in the lower forty-eight states.

As the sun went down, the snow melt snapped back into crystals, and the water stopped seeping into the soil. The freeze had returned. The bear slumped into a ball. Her heart rate slowed, and once more she slept. Gradually her breathing slowed down until she breathed only five times in two minutes. Bears are not true hibernators, for they can awaken if they must and go out to forage for food. On warm days in winter they sometimes get up and wander even if they're not hungry. For the most part, however, they sleep. They are semi-hibernators. The true hibernators cannot wake up until spring; their bodies become cold, their hearts barely beat, their breathing comes but once or twice a minute. Their awakening takes weeks and sometimes as long as a month. Among mammals the true hibernators include groundhogs, marmots, and some bats.

During the week after the first February thaw it became warm again. One morning the dripping and gurgling of the melt began before noon. The bear opened her eyes and cracked her cocoon wide open with her massive back and head. She rolled to her side and put her nose on the snow.

Two mourning doves were in a pine by the meadow. They had just returned from their winter home in Georgia and were quietly looking over their summer residence. It was at the edge of Tennessee's famous black bear country in the Smoky Mountains. Within the Appalachian mountain chain there is a steep ridge that runs from New York State to Alabama. All along the ridge the upland is speckled with inland swamps that the black bears seek for food, cover, and wallowing. The steep eastern front of the ridge is forested with bear staples: nut-bearing beech, hickory, and oak trees and fruit-bearing shrubs. At the bottom of the mountains are farms where apples

and peaches fall to the ground. This is a favorite habitat of the black bears. They also live in the swampy and wooded areas of the East, the mountains of the West, and all across Canada and Alaska to the Arctic Circle. In these bountiful habitats black bears meet, fight, raise young, and stuff themselves on nuts and berries until their coats shine.

The warm thaw of February ended when a cold front arrived from the North. It sent the sap down the trees and put the bear back to sleep. She rolled into a ball and snored. She was three years old and five feet long from her nose to her two-inch tail. When she stood on all fours, she was more than two feet high at the shoulder. She weighed two hundred pounds. She was black as space and as rugged as a boulder.

Last summer she had been the companion of the big three-hundred pound male black bear, or boar, who dominated all the other bears in the area. He was a fighter. His face and flank were scarred from battle, and one tooth was broken. He reigned over thousands of acres of forest, field, and roadside—and other bears. He stood as high as a bicycle's handles, and he had a neck as thick as a basketball hoop. Last July the big boar had met the young female bear as he strode across a meadow of flowers and raspberries. A younger male bear fled as the boar came on woofing and snorting. Frightened, the young female turned and ran. The boar growled. She stopped and looked back at him. He woofed to say she should come with him. She did.

She followed him among evening primroses into the night forest. She followed him along the top of the great ridge, then down a stream valley and into a campground. The boar signaled her to stop. She sat on her haunches. He walked past a tent where people were sleeping and, standing on his hind legs before a tall tree, reached up for a sweet-smelling ham. He could not reach it. It had been wired high to prevent just what the bear was attempting to do. This

did not discourage the big bear. Climbing swiftly with fore and back feet, much like a lineman, he grabbed the ham in his teeth. With a twist of his powerful neck he tore it free. It was as if it had been hung by cobwebs, not metal wires. The two bears devoured part of the ham, chewing and snarling while the people slept. They did not eat it all, for the wind brought the delicious scent of elderberries, which they much preferred to ham. The boar carried the ham for some distance, then abandoned it by a stream. It would be discovered the next day by crows and blue jays.

The next night the boar led the young female through dense hemlocks to a woodland meadow. There they ate cow parsnips and lilies. Although black bears will eat meat—a bit of a squirrel, an occasional mouse, frog, or snake—they primarily eat nuts, fruits, and berries. These foods create the mattress of fat they depend upon to get them through the foodless winter.

At dawn the wandering couple flopped down in a thicket and slept through the day.

On a warm summer night the boar came upon a wild bee tree. Rising to his hind feet, he pushed against it with his powerful forelegs. Three shoves and the old sycamore went down with a crash. Snarling and wheezing, he made splinters of the bee hollow with his teeth and claws. The enraged bees swarmed over him, stinging his nose, eyes, and ears to drive him off. The furry bear didn't even bother to swipe at them. He shredded the tree. The honeycombs spilled on the ground. Bouncing on the angry bees with his huge front paws, he woofed and wheezed until, defeated, they swarmed around their queen and departed. The two bears ate honey, bees, bees' eggs, larvae, and wax. When they had licked the last glob of honey from each other's shoulders and flanks, they rolled in the stream until their fur was clean. Their stomachs full, they went to their daytime bed in a hemlock grove. The day was hot, and they stretched out on their backs and snored.

During these summer days the bears became fast friends and then mates.

As the summer waned, the bears saw less and less of each other. One day in mid-August the big boar galloped up the mountain, pulled by the odor of ripening high bush blueberries on the ridge. The young female did not follow. She feasted on the jack-in-the-pulpit bulbs in the cool fern lands, wandered sunny fields, and swam back and forth across the stream to eat the berries on one side and the beech nuts and acorns on the other. By day she slept in a laurel grove beside a white cascade that roared over the edge of the ridge and plunged into the valley.

In the August moon of change she ate almost constantly, laying down the fat she would need for the winter. Even the late-autumn thunderstorms did not stop her from eating. As they rumbled over the Smoky Mountains and

filled the valleys with lightning and thunder, she went on eating nuts and berries.

In late September the first frost gripped the mountain. White ice crystals formed where there had been dew the day before. The cold tripped a biological timer within the bear, and drowsiness overcame her. She shuffled off to a fallen oak she had found last summer. Although some black bears just lie down under a bush or crawl into a cave or old groundhog den to sleep for the winter, the young bear scraped a saucer under the oak. The log was well hidden among laurel bushes and dense rhododendrons, birches, and hemlocks. Tangles of moosewood screened it from view.

The young bear made her den but did not go into it. She roamed the mountainside eating the abundant acorns at night and returned to sleep near the den by day.

The temperature dropped lower as the days shortened. The leaves stopped making green chlorophyll. As the chlorophyll faded, the red, yellow, orange, purple, and gold pigments in the leaves shone brightly. They painted the mountains with the festive colors of autumn. The birds departed for warmer climates, and the frogs and toads dug down into the mud and hibernated.

A snowstorm blew down on the mountain, and the young bear became so sleepy that she stopped eating. Sitting on her haunches beside the log, she waited for the signal from the earth that would send her off to bed. Her head drooped, her chunky body rocked from side to side, and her big black feet curled up at the toes. She dozed and awoke, but she did not go into her den.

One morning in November the air pressed down heavily upon her. The barometer was falling. The sky was dark, the valleys plunged in clouds. The wind whistled along the ridge, bringing snow. The flakes fell faster and faster. The bear sat by her den. The snow melted on her warm nose and fur. Still she did not go to

bed. The temperature dropped into the teens. A wild, blustery wind picked up the snow and drove it against trees and rocks. With that the bear got to her feet. Head down, eyes squinting, she walked to her den and went in. With sweeps of her paws she tossed leaves and sticks over herself, then slumped to her haunches. A bluebottle fly, too cold to move, fell from the underside of the log onto her fur and sat still. The wind and snow swirled on, covering the young bear's footprints so that there were no prints to tell where her den lay.

With sleepy movements she curled her head into her warm belly and put her front paws over her nose and her hind paws over her ears. With a sigh she closed her eyes. As the hours and days passed, she slipped off into the dark, faraway sleep of bear hibernation.

The signal that the bear had been waiting for was the storm. The frost and light snowstorms had made her sleepy, but it was the big storm that sent her to bed. It locked up the ridge of the Appalachians for the winter. All down the mountain chain where the storm had struck, the black bears went into their dens.

The young female did not feel the wind blow snow between the sticks and leaves she had pulled over herself. Time was standing still for the bear.

After the second thaw and freeze of February another thaw came to the mountain. The bear awoke and lay still with her eyes open. She twitched her nose to relieve an itch. The bluebottle fly had warmed up and was crawling along her big muzzle. It buzzed its wings. She shook her head. The cold air struck the bluebottle fly, and he dropped to her paw, too cold to move. She pulled her feet and head back into her den and dozed.

At noon the next day the bear felt moisture. The sap in the rhododendron was seeping out of a root she had cut open with her claws last autumn. In the noon thaw, the roots began taking up water and cell by cell, carrying it from

the wet ground to the bear's den. It moistened the ground. Softly growling, she pushed a bough under herself and shoved her shoulders out into the woods.

She wheezed and breathed more rapidly.

Under the bark of her log a ground beetle moved its wings. They crackled as the insect walked down a labyrinth it had chewed last summer. It stopped at a spot where the bark had fallen off in the winter. Here the air was so cold the beetle's jointed legs could not move. He had no choice but to stay where he was.

In a warmer spot in the log a bombardier beetle became mobile and walked up to a many-legged centipede that had awakened a day ago. The centipede sensed the approach of this inventive but fearsome beetle. The centipede reared and opened its poison claws to attack—too late. With a pop the bombardier turned around and shot a bullet of boiling-hot formic acid at the centipede. It crumpled and withered.

A young queen wasp was awakened by the thaw. She moved her antennae and walked a few steps to investigate her home in the log. She did not go far. The sun had moved far down the sky, and the freeze was returning. In moments the wasp could not move.

The bear felt the freeze and pulled back into her den. The sun went down. The sap stopped running and slid back into the roots of the bushes and trees. Droplets of water froze, and the bear drifted back to sleep once more.

In the middle of the night she awoke. Murmuring to herself, she rolled from side to side, growled, and went back to sleep.

Before noon the next day she shuffled out of her den a few yards and stretched out on the snow. She smelled greenery. Digging with her two-inch-long foreclaws, she uncovered a chickweed. Her tongue rolled out, and she ate the lowly plant that was blooming under the leaves and ice. Near the chickweed the leaves of the hepatica were growing. The nubby heads of the wood violets were above the ground. The early-blooming plants were racing toward the sunlight. The snow and the leaves were helping them grow. Like a greenhouse the snow held the heat from the decomposing leaves around the flowers.

The bluebottle fly felt the raw air and walked deeper into the bear's warm fur.

When the sun reached its apogee, the steel-gray tips of the hardwood trees glowed pink. The sap had reached them that day, and they were swelling and bringing the first color to the mountain range.

The sad cooing of a mourning dove floated down from the pine tree near the meadow. Presently the male alighted on a limb of the pine tree with a twig in his bill. His mate was looking at a stick she had placed on the limb. It wobbled and almost fell. The male put his twig beside it and both lay still. The doves touched beaks. A few more sticks and their nest would be ready for the two eggs the female would lay.

The nest was not well constructed compared to other birds' nests, but it was still an inspiration to the male. At the sight of it he flew up in the air. His wings clacked as they struck each other above his back. He climbed one hundred feet above the nearby meadow and, on motionless wings, soared earthward. He sped downward in a sweeping arc, his wings held low. As he fell, the white on his tail glowed and his feathers clattered. Seconds before he landed beside his mate, he flapped his wings and slowed down. She cooed. He had flown the love dance of the mourning dove. Their eggs would be laid before the February moon had waned.

The bear awoke just enough to hear the crows caw as they flew in pairs through the trees. The moon of February had scattered their youngsters over the hills to find mates of their own. The old pair flew over their property.

Voices calling from the swamp crackled, *quong-ker-chie*. The male red-winged blackbirds were back from the south. The females would join them in a week or ten days. Four males arrived in the bear's swamp on this, the first wave of their spring migration. More would fly tomorrow. Then hundreds, thousands, and millions would fly up the Atlantic Flyway, the migration route of the birds on the East Coast. Some would stay in the Smoky Mountains, and millions would fan out to the North. A few of these would go on to the MacKenzie River in the Northwest Territories. An occasional pair would turn up in Alaska.

While the bear lolled on the snow, a chickadee sang half of his love song. A cardinal sang a brief part of his song. The moon of February is a time of awakening and slumbering for the birds as well as the bears. The longer hours of sunlight bring them into their bright breeding plumage and into song. On the days of the thaw they carol a few snatches of their territorial songs. These short beautiful arias are followed by long silences during the moon of the bears.

The temperature dropped below freezing, and the bear got slowly to her feet and walked back into her den. The bluebottle fly went with her.

Snow fell; the cold deepened. The sap did not run. The mourning doves sat on their limb and pulled their feet into their feathers. The chickadees hid in hollows. The bluebottle fly crawled into the bear's fur and held its wings close to its back. Life in the forests slowed. The winter was not over.

On the night of the waning quarter moon, westerly winds blew the storm to sea and cleared the sky. The stars and moon shone clearly. The bear snored. In a nearby sweet gum tree, a raccoon poked his head out of his doorway and sniffed. He pulled his head in. A few minutes later he looked out again and, clutching the tree trunk with his hind and front feet, walked to the ground headfirst. Gingerly he stepped onto the cold snow. He was restless tonight. Chuttering softly, he trekked off.

Nearing a sycamore tree, he smelled the scents of the home where he had been born and started up the tree. He never reached the old hollow. His father was leaning out of the hole, snarling and growling. The raccoon laid back his ears, jumped into the snow, and was gone.

He stopped in a grove of sassafras. The trees smelled pungent and clean. Suddenly another raccoon jumped on him. He reared to fight. It was a pert female raccoon. She ran around him, bit his ringed tail, and finally sat down and looked at him. With a chutter she got up and walked through the snow. He followed her over a boulder and down between tall spruce trees to an old hollow willow. She leaped to the trunk and, clinging there, sniffed down at him. He nipped her black heels. She dropped to the ground and jumped on him. She ran. He ran. She kicked up the snow. He kicked up the snow. Finally she galloped up the willow and climbed into her hollow. He followed her, for it was February, the time when raccoons pick mates.

Many nights later the raccoon came back from a fishing expedition. He climbed the willow as he had always done and started down the inside of the hollow to find the pert female. She snarled at him and bared her teeth. The mating of the raccoons was over. The little female would raise their offspring alone. They would be born in sixty-three days, when the crayfish and frogs were plentiful.

The raccoon backed up, scrambled down the tree, and returned to his own den. He went back to sleep. Like the bear, he had laid down a layer of fat that would keep him warm and sustain him until spring.

On the night of the last phase of the moon, the temperature dropped well below freezing. Nevertheless, the young bear woke up. Her heart beat steadily, and her breathing became normal.

With a rolling moan, and still half asleep, she

felt her abdomen muscles tighten. She gave birth to a small, wet cub. She cleaned it lovingly until its black fur was dry and standing upright. Its eyes and ears were closed, and its back legs were limp. They would not develop into sturdy legs until it was time for the cub to walk safely out of the den and not get lost.

The cub was tiny, about as big as a person's hand, and weighed only eight ounces, the weight of a small jar of mustard. Blind, deaf, and feeble, it knew exactly what to do. It climbed up its mother's stomach to her mammae and nursed. While it snuggled in her warm black fur, she gave birth to another cub. When both were cuddled against her, she put her front paws around them, curled her head and chest over them, pulled her hind feet up over her head, and went back to sleep.

The moon of the bears had seen the birth of two beautiful cubs. They would suckle and sleep in their mother's arms until May, when the moon of rebirth was upon the land.

On a warm night in that month the young mother bear would lead two fuzzy, five-pound cubs out of the den into the woods. They would smell the new leaves, the busy insects, and the meadow beyond their den. They would investigate boulders and rhododendron bushes. They would tremble a little at the strange vastness of the mountain.

When they were comfortable with their surroundings, the handsome mother would walk slowly along the ridge and proudly show off her beautiful cubs to the wild community.

On that day the bluebottle fly would leave the bear den and fly to the stream. There she would lay eggs in the last bit of rotting ham, another reminder of last summer's events.

Bibliography

Ahlstrom, Mark E. *The Black Bear.* Mankato, Minn.: Crestwood House, 1985.

Bailey, Bernadine. *Wonders of the World of Bears.* New York: Dodd, Mead, 1981.

Burt, William Henry, and Richard Philip Grossenheider. *A Field Guide to the Mammals.* The Peterson Field Guide Series. Boston: Houghton Mifflin, 1976.

Buxton, Jane Heath. *Baby Bears and How They Grow.* Washington, D.C.: National Geographic Society, 1986.

Ford, Barbara. *Black Bear: The Spirit of the Wilderness.* Boston: Houghton Mifflin, 1981.

Graham, Ada. *Bears in the Wild.* New York: Delacorte, 1987.

Johnson, Fred. *The Big Bears.* Washington, D.C.: National Wildlife Federation, 1977.

McPhee, John. "A Textbook Place for Bears." *The New Yorker,* December 27, 1982, page 42.

Moon, Cliff. *Bears in the Wild.* Hove, England: Wayland, 1985.

Morey, Walter. *Operation Blue Bear.* New York: Dutton, 1975.

Pringle, Laurence P. *Bearman: Exploring the World of Black Bears.* New York: Scribner, 1989.

Index

Alaska, 14, 18, 37
Appalachian Mountains, 9, 12, 16, 29
Arctic Circle, 14, 18

bee, 22
beech tree, 16
beetle, 32
birch tree, 12, 25
blueberry, 23
bluebottle fly, 28, 29, 34, 38, 44
blue jay, 12, 21
bombardier beetle, 32

California, 14, 25
Canada, 9, 14, 18
cardinal, 37
centipede, 32
chickadee, 37, 38
chickweed, 33
conifers, 10
crow, 21, 36

elderberry, 21

Florida, 12

Georgia, 9, 16
grizzly bear, 14–15
ground beetle, 32

hemlock tree, 10, 21, 22, 25
hepatica, 33

hickory tree, 16
honey, 22

jack-in-the-pulpit, 23

laurel bush, 23, 25

maple tree, 12
moosewood, 25
mourning dove, 16, 34–36, 38

oak tree, 10, 16, 25
Oregon, 14

pine trees, 10, 34
polar bear, 14

raccoon, 38–40
red-winged blackbird, 36–37
rhododendron, 25, 29, 44
Rocky Mountains, 14

sassafras, 39
Smoky Mountains, 16, 23, 37
spruce tree, 10, 39
sweet gum tree, 38
sycamore tree, 39

Tennessee, 10, 16

violet, 34

Washington, 14
wasp, 33
white grubs, 12